Happy Birthday, Good Knight

BY Shelley Moore Thomas
PICTURES BY Jennifer Plecas

DUTTON CHILDREN'S BOOKS

DUTTON CHILDREN'S BOOKS
A division of Penguin Young Readers Group

Published by the Penguin Group
Penguin Group (USA) Inc., 375 Hudson Street, New York, New York 10014, U.S.A • Penguin Group (Canada), 90 Eglinton Avenue East, Suite 700, Toronto, Ontario, Canada M4P 2Y3 (a division of Pearson Penguin Canada Inc.) Penguin Books Ltd, 80 Strand, London WC2R 0RL, England • Penguin Ireland, 25 St Stephen's Green, Dublin 2, Ireland (a division of Penguin Books Ltd) Penguin Group (Australia), 250 Camberwell Road, Camberwell, Victoria 3124, Australia (a division of Pearson Australia Group Pty Ltd) • Penguin Books India Pvt Ltd, 11 Community Centre, Panchsheel Park, New Delhi - 110 017, India Penguin Group (NZ), Cnr Airborne and Rosedale Roads, Albany, Auckland 1310, New Zealand (a division of Pearson New Zealand Ltd) • Penguin Books (South Africa) (Pty) Ltd, 24 Sturdee Avenue, Rosebank, Johannesburg 2196, South Africa Penguin Books Ltd, Registered Offices: 80 Strand, London WC2R 0RL, England

Library of Congress Cataloging-in-Publication Data
Thomas, Shelley Moore.
Happy birthday, Good Knight / by Shelley Moore Thomas;
pictures by Jennifer Plecas.
p. cm.
Summary: The Good Knight tries to help three little dragons make
a birthday present for a very special friend.
ISBN 0-525-47184-7 (hardcover)
[1. Knights and knighthood—Fiction. 2. Dragons—Fiction. 3. Gifts—Fiction.
4. Birthdays—Fiction.] I. Plecas, Jennifer, ill. II. Title.
PZ7.T369453Hap 2005 [E]—dc22 2005009592

Published in the United States by Dutton Children's Books,
a division of Penguin Young Readers Group
345 Hudson Street, New York, New York 10014
www.penguin.com/youngreaders

Manufactured in China • First Edition

10 9 8 7 6 5 4 3 2 1

For J.B. III

S.M.T.

For Maggie, with thanks

J.P.

The sun was rising
over the deep dark forest.
Inside a cozy cave there
lived three little dragons.
They were talking with their friend
the Good Knight.

“We have a problem,”

said the first dragon.

“We need to get

a birthday gift,”

said the second dragon.

“For someone very special,”

said the third dragon.

"But we don't have any money.
What can we do?"
asked all three dragons.
The Good Knight thought and thought.
"Aha!" he said. "Methinks I know."

"The most special gifts
do not come from a store.
They come from
our hearts and our hands,
nothing more," said the Good Knight.
"What does that mean?"
asked all three dragons.

“The best gifts are the ones
we make ourselves,”
said the Good Knight.
“Will you help us? Please?”
asked the dragons.
The Good Knight did not
know what to think.

But he was a good knight.

"Come with me," he said.

The Good Knight hitched up the cart.

The dragons got in.

He jumped on his horse.

Clippety-clop. Clippety-clop.

They went through the deep dark forest to the Good Knight's crumbly tumbly tower.

"We will make a cake,"

said the Good Knight.

"Everybody loves cake!"

In the Good Knight's kitchen
the work began.
The dragons made a double-layer,
double-chocolate,
double-swirl cake
with sparkly sprinkles on top.
At least they tried to.

But three little dragons
in one little kitchen
can make one big mess.
"I don't believe this!"
said the Good Knight.
There was flour on the ceiling,
sugar on the chairs,
cake batter on the floor,
and sprinkles everywhere.

"This is a wreck!" cried the Good Knight.

He got the clean-up buckets

and soapy soapsuds.

He got the brooms and brushes.

The dragons scrubbed the ceiling.

Scrubby, scrubby, scrubby.

The dragons swept the floor.

Swish, swish, swish.

They even washed the seats of the chairs.

Brush-a, brush-a, brush-a.

They cleaned until the little kitchen was

C-L-E-A-N.

“We still have a problem,”
said the dragons.
“We still don’t have a birthday
gift for someone very special.”
And they began to cry
drippy droppy dragon tears.

The Good Knight did not

know what to think.

But he was a good knight.

So he came up with a new idea.

"Don't cry, good dragons,"

said the Good Knight.

"We will make a birthday card.

Everybody loves birthday cards!"

In the Good Knight's study,
the work began.
The little dragons made a giant
pop-up birthday card
with shimmery, glimmery rainbows.
At least they tried to.

But three little dragons

in one little study

can make one big mess.

"I don't believe this!"

cried the Good Knight.

There was paint on the ceiling,

glue on the chairs, paper on the floor,

and glitter everywhere.

And the pop-up card was glued shut.

"This is a ruin!"

cried the Good Knight.

He got the clean-up buckets

and soapy soapsuds.

He got the brooms

and brushes.

The dragons scrubbed the ceiling.

Scrubby, scrubby, scrubby.

The dragons swept the floor.

Swish, swish, swish.

They even washed the seats of the chairs.

Brush-a, brush-a, brush-a.

They cleaned until the study was

C-L-E-A-N.

“We still don’t have a birthday gift
for someone very special,”
said the dragons.
And they began to cry
drippy droppy dragon tears.
The Good Knight did not
know what to think.

But he was a good knight.

And he got another good idea.

"We will put on a magic show.

Everybody loves magic!" he said.

In the Good Knight's sitting room,

the work began.

The dragons planned a flashy, splashy magic show with balloon animals, bright colored streamers, and birds that flew away. At least they tried to.

But three little dragons

in one little sitting room

can make one big mess.

"I don't believe this!"

cried the Good Knight.

There were feathers on the ceiling,

streamers on the chairs,

bits of paper on the floor,

and popped balloons everywhere.

"This is a disaster!"

he cried.

He got the clean-up buckets

and soapy soapsuds.

He got the brooms

and brushes.

The dragons scrubbed the ceiling.

Scrubby, scrubby, scrubby.

The dragons swept the floor.

Swish, swish, swish.

They even washed the seats of the chairs.

Brush-a, brush-a, brush-a.

They cleaned until the sitting room was

C-L-E-A-N.

The Good Knight sat down
at his little kitchen table.
It was very late.
He was very tired.

The clock struck midnight.

"Oh no!" cried the little dragons.
"Now it is too late!"

The dragons began to cry
drippy droppy dragon tears.

"Today was your birthday.
We wanted the birthday gift for you.
Now it is too late," said the dragons.

The Good Knight looked at his calendar.

Yes, indeed, it was

his birthday.

He began to smile.

Then he giggled and laughed.

"You have given me the best gift there is,"

he said.

The dragons did not

know what to think.

"We did not make a cake

or a card or a magic show.

We only made big fat messes,"

they said.

"You made something else.
You made me laugh!"
said the Good Knight.
"The gift of laughter
is the best gift there is!"
The dragons thought of
the big fat messes.

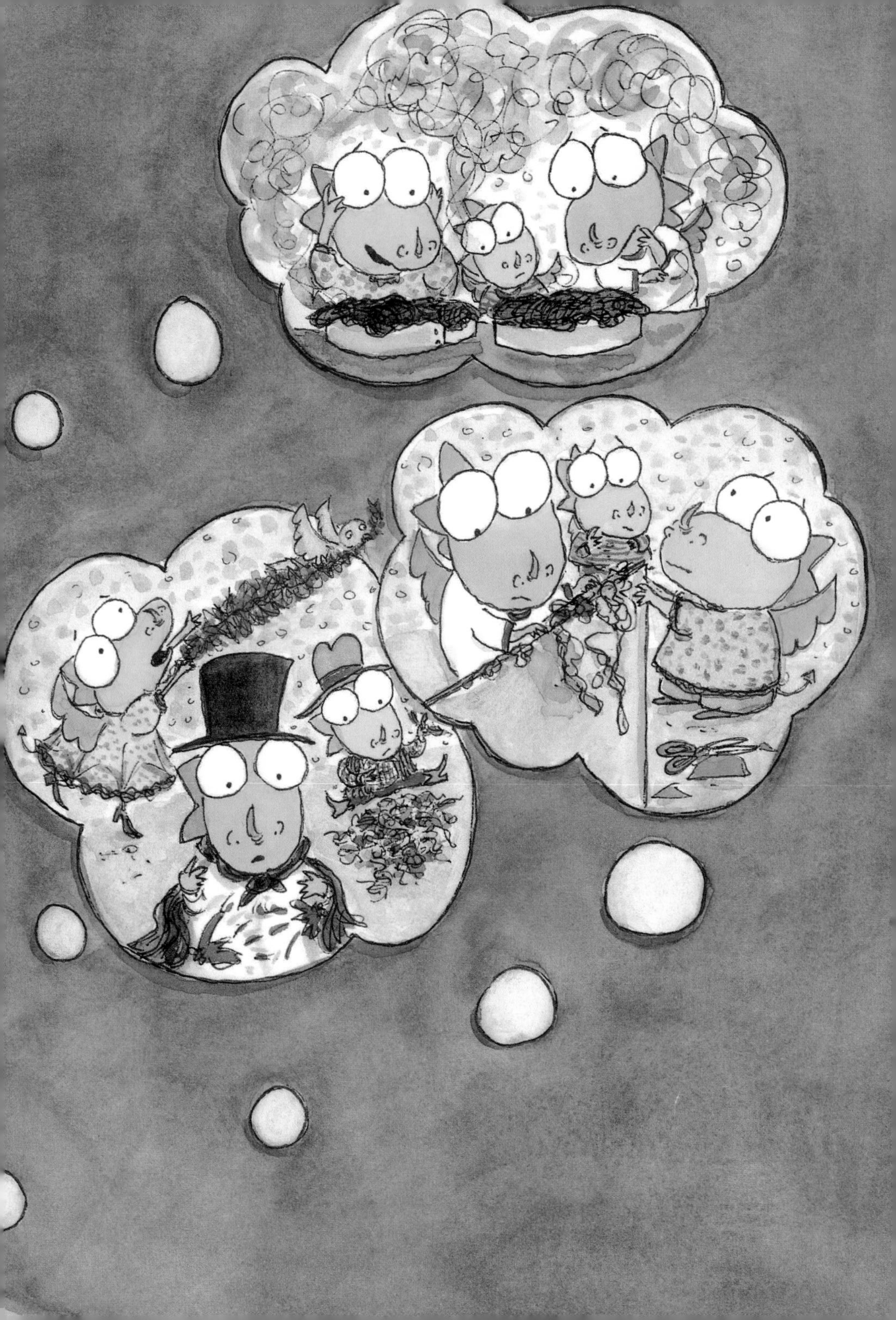

They began to smile.

They giggled and laughed.

They laughed until the

drippy droppy dragon tears

were all gone.

"Yes, little dragons.
I will never forget this day,"
said the Good Knight.

Then the Good Knight and the three little dragons ate the burnt cake.

The Good Knight opened his sticky, gluey card.

The dragons did a magic trick.

Then the dragons began to sing:

"Happy birthday to you.

Happy birthday to you.

Happy birthday, Good Knight.

Happy birthday to you!"

“Thank you, good dragons,”

said the Good Knight.

“It was a good birthday.”